Words to Know Before You Read

aboard

captain

cheerful

coaxed

complained

enjoyed

exercise

gratefully

motion

whined

www.rourkeeducationalmedia.com

Edited by Precious McKenzie
Illustrated by Anita DuFalla
Art Direction and Page Layout by Renee Brady

Library of Congress PCN Data

Keep Your Chin Up / Colleen Hord
ISBN 978-1-61810-182-2 (hard cover) (alk. paper)
ISBN 978-1-61810-315-4 (soft cover)
Library of Congress Control Number: 2012936783

Rourke Educational Media
Printed in the United States of America,
North Mankato, Minnesota

rourkeeducationalmedia.com
customerservice@rourkeeducationalmeida.com • PO Box 643328 Vero Beach, Florida 32964

Keep Your Chin Up

By Colleen Hord

Illustrated by Anita DuFalla

Calypso, a happy cat, lived aboard a pirate ship. Calypso shared the ship with three other cats and the ship's captain.

Unlike Calypso, the other cats complained about everything. This made the captain sad.

"Are we there yet?" they whined.

"We are tired of eating smelly fish!" they grumbled. "We would like to try something different to eat."

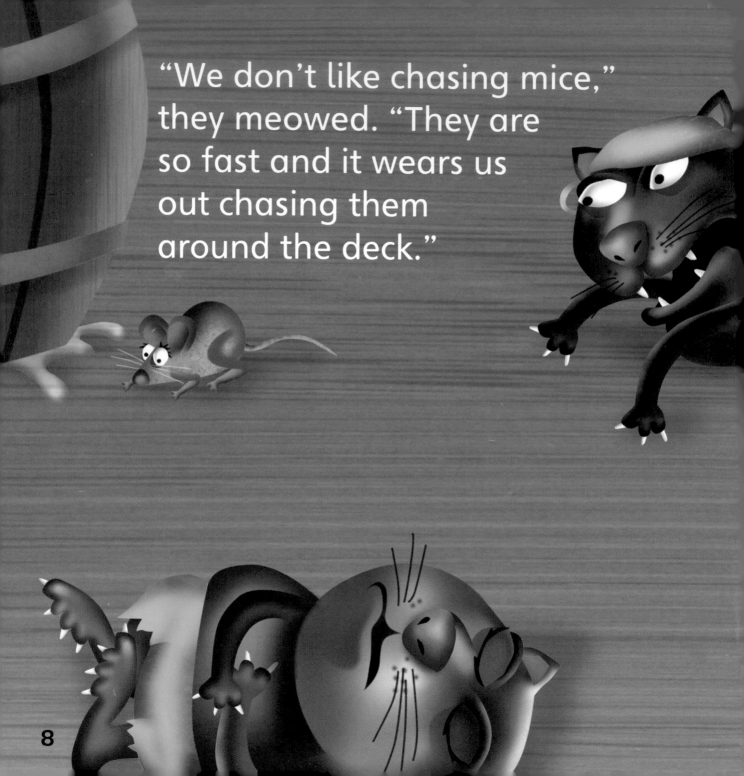

"We don't like chasing mice," they meowed. "They are so fast and it wears us out chasing them around the deck."

Calypso never complained.
She kept her chin up
and stayed cheerful,
no matter what.

9

She liked the motion of the ocean. The waves rocked her to sleep every night.

She enjoyed chasing the mice.
She knew how much the captain
needed the mice to stay at bay.

She purred gratefully after every meal of fish. Calypso knew that some cats in the world were hungry.

One night, after the other cats had complained all day long, Calypso called a cat meeting.

"Every day you complain and complain and complain. I can't take it anymore," she said.

"You need to focus on the good things in your lives. You don't look up to see the open sky."

15

"You aren't thankful for your fish dinner. You are lucky to have plenty of food to eat every day."

"You forget that the captain needs you to keep the mice at bay."

17

"Please try to be happy and quit complaining," coaxed Calypso.

The other cats looked at each other. They thought for a while.

18

"Maybe she's right," said the yellow cat.
"There is a lot of good in the world."

"I do like the fresh sea air," meowed the black cat.

"Chasing mice can be good exercise," said the gray cat.

With Calypso's help, the other cats started seeing the good things in their lives. They stopped complaining and started purring. The captain started smiling again. They sailed the high seas together for many happy years.

After Reading Activities

You and the Story...

Which of the characters would you like for a friend? Explain your answer.

Would you want to live on a ship?

What lesson do you think the other cats learned from Calypso?

Words You Know Now...

On another piece of paper, find the root, or main part, of each word. Pick three of the words you find, and for each word, write a sentence.

aboard
captain
cheerful
coaxed
complained

enjoyed
exercise
gratefully
motion
whined

You Could...Change the Setting of the Story

- Write your own version of Keep Your Chin Up with a different setting.

- Where else could this story take place?

- How would you have to change what the cats said to fit your setting?

- How would the ending change using your new setting?

About the Author

Colleen Hord is an elementary school teacher. Her favorite part of her teaching day is Writer's Workshop. She enjoys kayaking, camping, walking on the beach, and reading in her hammock.

Ask The Author!
www.rem4students.com

About the Illustrator

Acclaimed for its versatility in style, Anita DuFalla's work has appeared in many educational books, newspaper articles, and business advertisements and on numerous posters, book and magazine covers, and even giftwraps. Anita's passion for pattern is evident in both her artwork and her collection of 400 patterned tights. She lives in the Friendship neighborhood of Pittsburgh, Pennsylvania with her son, Lucas.